Jonathan de la

Coconut Dreams

Written by: Jonathan de la Rosa

Illustrated by: Russel Dos Ramos and Jonathan de la Rosa

ISBN: 978-976-8239-42-6

Layout: Paria Publishing Co. Ltd.
Printed in China

It was a beautiful, sunny afternoon in Jelly Bay.

Husky and Daddy Coconutree had been building sandcastles all day.

I have other great plans as well, pops.
I would like to do so much more.
Before Daddy Coconutree could say a word,
Husky let his imagination soar.

I will travel the universe,
and be the first coconut to walk on the moon.

Winning the Coconut Open,
beating the world's number one by four.

To be a great explorer
will bring me much pleasure.

Combing the oceans' floors in search of sunken treasure.

I shall travel the seas in search of the biggest fish.

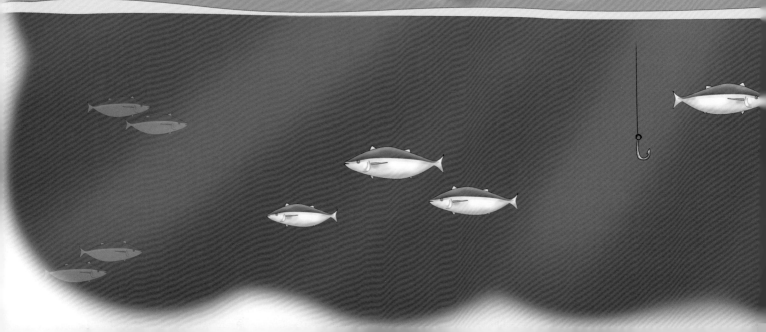

To catch one over a thousand pounds;
this would be my greatest wish.

What about a famous pan player, Daddy? That might be cool!

I could become a pan professor, and start my very own pan school.

Daddy Coconutree just smiled as Husky rambled on.

That's it, Daddy!
A pannist... with a number one song.

Be honest and true. Always give of your best.
That is all we ask of you:
Nothing more... nothing less.

The End.

Books in this series:

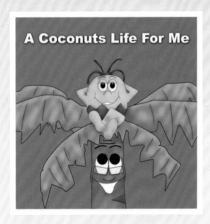

Look out for Husky's next adventure!